Books by Jacqueline Harvey

Clementine Rose and the Surprise Visitor
Clementine Rose and the Pet Day Disaster
Clementine Rose and the Perfect Present
Clementine Rose and the Farm Fiasco
Clementine Rose and the Seaside Escape
Clementine Rose and the Treasure Box
Clementine Rose and the Famous Friend
Clementine Rose and the Ballet Break-In

Alice-Miranda at School
Alice-Miranda on Holiday
Alice-Miranda Takes the Lead
Alice-Miranda at Sea
Alice-Miranda in New York
Alice-Miranda Shows the Way
Alice-Miranda in Paris
Alice-Miranda Shines Bright
Alice-Miranda in Japan
Alice-Miranda at Camp
Alice-Miranda at the Palace

CLEMENTINE ROSE

and the Movie Magic

Jacqueline Harvey

RANDOM HOUSE AUSTRALIA

A Random House book
Published by Random House Australia Pty Ltd
Level 3, 100 Pacific Highway, North Sydney NSW 2060
www.randomhouse.com.au

Penguin
Random House
RANDOM HOUSE BOOKS

First published by Random House Australia in 2015

Random House Books is part of the Penguin Random House group of
companies whose addresses can be found at global.penguinrandomhouse.com.

National Library of Australia
Cataloguing-in-Publication Entry

Author: Harvey, Jacqueline
Title: Clementine Rose and the movie magic/Jacqueline Harvey
ISBN: 978 0 85798 518 7 (pbk)
Series: Harvey, Jacqueline. Clementine Rose; 9
Target audience: For primary school age
Subjects: Girls – Juvenile fiction
        Motion pictures – Juvenile fiction
Dewey number: A823.4

Cover and internal illustrations by J.Yi
Cover design and additional illustration by Leanne Beattie
Internal design by Midland Typesetters
Typeset in ITC Century 12.5/19 by Midland Typesetters, Australia
Printed in Australia by Griffin Press, an accredited ISO AS/NZS
14001:2004 Environmental Management System printer

Random House Australia uses papers that are natural, renewable and
recyclable products and made from wood grown in sustainable forests.
The logging and manufacturing processes are expected to conform to
the environmental regulations of the country of origin.

*For Phoebe Rose and
her big brothers and sister,
Darcy, Flynn and Eden, and for Ian,
who shares this magical journey with me*

LIGHTS, CAMERA, ACTION!

Clementine Rose stood on the middle of the front stairs, practising her lines.

'How did that sound, Grandpa?' She looked up at the portrait of her grandfather, which hung on the wall beside the painting of her grandmother. 'Basil said that we can start again if I make a mistake.'

'Godfathers, I don't know why you bother,' Clementine's Great-Aunt Violet said, striding down from the top floor. 'He's not said a word in years, at least not to me.'

Clementine giggled. 'I still like talking to him, anyway – and to Granny. She's got the loveliest smile.'

Aunt Violet paused for a moment to stare at the faces of her brother and sister-in-law. A strange pain clawed at her chest and she winced.

'Are you all right?' Clementine looked up at the woman's watery blue eyes.

Violet Appleby brushed at the side of her face. 'Yes, yes. I'm fine. I just haven't thought about Edmund and Davina much recently. You're right, though – your grandmother did have a lovely smile.'

The woman turned to Clementine and promptly changed the subject.

'Are you ready?' she asked.

Clementine nodded. 'I think so, except for the butterflies having a boxing match in my tummy.'

'Well, you tell them to calm right down,' Aunt Violet instructed. 'Take a few deep breaths and you'll be fine.'

The child had been looking forward to this moment for weeks. Ever since she landed a starring role in their neighbour Basil Hobbs's documentary about Penberthy House, Clementine had counted down the days until the end of the school term, when filming was scheduled to begin. While her mother and Uncle Digby had both helped Clemmie to learn her lines, it was Aunt Violet who had made sure that she was word perfect.

Clementine was very good at remembering things off by heart. It had started when she was much younger, when Uncle Digby would teach her poems which she would then recite for Granny and Grandpa. But this was different. This time there was a camera to capture her every move.

Clementine peered over the banister into the entrance foyer below. Basil was talking to her mother while fiddling with a huge movie camera on a tripod. He wore a bright-yellow waistcoat and a matching bow tie with red spots on it. Clementine thought Basil looked even more stylish than usual, particularly with the addition of a navy beret, which he'd told her was his lucky director's hat.

Close by, a tall man wearing a large set of headphones fiddled with a long stick that had a furry microphone attached to its end. A small boy with dark-brown hair stood beside him, watching his every move.

Basil looked up at Clementine and waggled his eyebrows excitedly. 'We're almost ready. Would you like to join us downstairs, Aunt Violet? You can watch from here.'

Clementine was wearing a pretty navy-blue dress and her favourite red patent Mary Jane shoes. Mrs Mogg, the owner of the village shop, had made the dress especially for the occasion.

Aunt Violet gave the child a quick once-over and adjusted the red ribbon in her hair. 'Perfect,' she said with a wink.

Clementine lunged forward and hugged the old woman around her middle. 'Thank you for helping me. I really 'preciate it,' the child said.

'The word is *a*-ppreciate, Clementine,' Violet Appleby tutted, making her way down the stairs. 'One of these days I'll teach you to speak the Queen's English.'

Clementine looked at Basil, awaiting his instruction.

'In a minute I'll snap the board and call "action",' he explained. 'You can start anytime you like.'

'Okay,' the child replied. 'But are you sure I can do it again if I make a mistake?'

'Of course,' Basil said with a nod. 'And remember to enjoy yourself. I always do!'

Clementine grinned.

'Good luck, sweetheart,' Lady Clarissa called. 'You'll be wonderful.'

Digby Pertwhistle walked into the hallway and stood beside Aunt Violet. The pair of them smiled up at Clementine.

'Penberthy House introduction, take one . . . Action!' Basil called before snapping the clapperboard like a castanet.

Clementine took a deep breath and looked directly into the camera. 'Hello, my name is Clementine Rose Appleby and this is my home, Penberthy House Hotel. When my granny and grandpa were alive –' Clementine looked up at the portraits of her grandparents on the wall, then back at the camera – 'it was just Penberthy House without the hotel.

These days we have lots of guests coming and going. It's the best place to live in the whole wide world, especially since we got the new roof and we don't have to put buckets out every time it rains.' Clementine gave a small grin. 'I hope you love learning about our house as much as I love living –'

Just as Clementine was about to finish the sentence the telephone in the hallway rang.

'Cut!' Basil called out.

Lady Clarissa apologised and ran to answer it.

'Why didn't you take it off the hook, Pertwhistle?' Aunt Violet glared at Uncle Digby. 'Honestly.'

The man ignored her.

Clementine looked over the banister at Basil and the others.

'That was fabulous, Clemmie.' Basil gave her two thumbs up. 'We'll do it again once your mother comes back.'

Clementine nodded.

It was quite a while before Lady Clarissa returned to the group, and when she did her face was flushed.

'Are you all right, Mummy?' Clementine asked.

'Yes, of course, darling.' The woman gave a pinched smile.

Aunt Violet arched an eyebrow at her niece. 'You don't fool me, Clarissa,' she whispered. 'What was that about?'

Lady Clarissa lowered her voice. 'It was the local council. It seems they've received an anonymous complaint about Penberthy House. They're sending their Health and Safety Inspector to do a full assessment of the hotel.'

'I'm sure it's nothing to worry about,' Uncle Digby reassured her in hushed tones. 'When is the inspection?'

Clarissa winced. 'Tomorrow.'

'Tomorrow!' Aunt Violet exclaimed. 'That doesn't work at all. We're shooting a movie.'

'I tried to put them off but they insisted,' Lady Clarissa said helplessly.

'Well, surely the inspector will only be here for the day,' Aunt Violet said.

'I'm afraid we've got Mr Doncaster for as many days as he needs to be certain of his findings,' Clarissa replied.

'That's ridiculous!' Aunt Violet huffed. 'Clearly the council enjoy paying people to have holidays. I'll take care of him. You know I can be utterly charming when required.'

'Clearly that's not required very often,' Digby mumbled.

Aunt Violet shot the man a look that would have stopped a charging rhino in its tracks.

Clementine wondered what her mother and Uncle Digby and Aunt Violet were talking about. Whatever it was had given them all frowny faces.

'Ready, Clementine?' Basil called out.

The child nodded. A tiny flutter tickled her tummy again.

Basil held up the clapperboard. 'All right, everyone. Penberthy House introduction, take two . . . Action!'

BOOKING BUNGLE

'So how did you enjoy your first day on set, Clementine?' Basil Hobbs's eyes sparkled as he sipped his tea.

Filming had finally wrapped for the day and Basil, his sound engineer and assistant cameraman, Drew, and Drew's seven-year-old son, Will, were enjoying afternoon tea in the kitchen with the Appleby household.

'I loved it!' Clementine replied, her blue eyes as round as saucers. 'But I didn't know it would take so many times to get it right.'

Drew looked across at the girl. 'That's because Basil is a perfectionist. Not only does he make great movies, he's like Sherlock Holmes when it comes to sniffing out the facts. If there are any skeletons hidden in the Appleby closet he's bound to find them,' Drew said with a wink.

Aunt Violet shifted uncomfortably in her seat.

'We have a skeleton,' Clementine said matter-of-factly, 'but it's in the attic, not the closet.'

The adults grinned. 'That's not quite what Basil meant, Clemmie,' her mother said.

Basil nodded. 'I just don't see the point in doing something if you're not going to give it your best.'

Clementine bit her lip and wondered if Basil really was happy with her performance that day. Her introduction had been filmed another twelve times before he'd decided he had exactly what he needed. The group had then moved into the sitting room to film a short scene. Even though Clementine had only a couple of lines of dialogue, they had done seven takes before Basil was satisfied.

'And you, my dear girl, gave it your best and more,' Basil added enthusiastically.

Clementine beamed and all doubts about her performance disappeared.

'Can I pour you some more tea, Drew?' Clarissa offered.

'That would be lovely, thanks,' he replied.

As Drew reached for another plump scone, he accidentally brushed Clarissa's hand and a spark of static electricity passed between them. The woman jumped, spilling tea all over the tablecloth.

'Oops!' Drew grabbed his napkin and mopped up the liquid. He smiled at Clarissa, whose cheeks blushed a fiery red.

Uncle Digby and Aunt Violet raised their eyebrows at one another. Clementine spotted their funny looks and hoped they weren't about to start squabbling.

Basil thumbed through a thick wad of papers in front of him. 'We'll start at nine in the morning, and I'll need Clementine dressed as her great-great grandmother, Clarissa,' he said.

'How exactly is this film going to play out, Basil?' Violet Appleby asked. She placed her teacup back onto its saucer with a rattle.

The man looked up from his notes. 'I have a rough plan. Some of the old family papers have given me ideas, although it would have been wonderful to find a diary and include a few more anecdotes in the film.'

'I was sure Granny had one,' Lady Clarissa said, 'but I've searched everywhere and I can't find a thing.'

'Never mind,' Basil said. 'Having Clementine narrate various sections allows me to intro- duce the different generations of the Appleby family who have lived in the house. In answer to your question, Aunt Violet, today we filmed Clementine as herself, but tomorrow she's going to play the role of her great-great grandmother. I think it's Thursday that she's pretending to be you, although we're taking some poetic licence with that one. It's a pity there are no photographs of you as a child.'

'I don't remember there ever being many. I suspect, being a girl, I wasn't interesting enough,' Aunt Violet explained with a flick of her hand.

Clarissa gave the woman a quizzical look. She'd found plenty of pictures of her father when he was a boy and she couldn't imagine that her grandparents only took photographs of their son. Though, she had searched the house from top to bottom and had been very disappointed to find just a couple of snaps of Aunt Violet as a baby. It seemed quite odd, really.

'What did you look like when you were little, Aunt Violet?' Clementine asked.

The old woman snorted. 'How would I know, Clementine? I didn't spend all day looking at myself, did I?'

'Really?' Uncle Digby teased. 'I don't think I've ever seen you walk past a mirror without sneaking a glance.'

'Very funny, Pertwhistle,' Aunt Violet quipped. 'Perhaps you should try looking in one occasionally.'

'If that portrait on the stairs is anything to go by, you were extremely pretty,' Drew said.

Aunt Violet smothered a smile. 'Oh, Drew, don't be so silly.'

'Yes, Drew, don't be so silly,' Uncle Digby parroted.

Aunt Violet gave the butler a withering look.

'So how long have you two been married?' Drew asked, looking at Aunt Violet and Uncle Digby.

The old woman sputtered her tea and Uncle Digby went green. 'Married!' they wheezed in unison.

Drew grimaced. 'Sorry, I didn't mean to offend anyone.'

To everyone's relief, the front doorbell rang. Digby Pertwhistle shot up from his chair and went to see who it was.

Clementine looked over at Drew. His hair was the colour of salt and pepper, and he smiled with his eyes. When he laughed, Clementine thought it sounded like church bells ringing.

'Do you like working on movies?' she asked him.

The man nodded. 'I started running around with a camera when I was just a bit older than you, and I can't imagine doing anything else. In fact, Will has just started making movies too.'

'Really?' Clementine's eyes widened.

The boy gave a small nod. 'I could teach you,' he said quietly.

'Would you?' Clementine asked brightly, then frowned. 'But we don't have a video camera.'

'Didn't you win one earlier this year, Clarissa?' Aunt Violet reminded her niece.

'Oh, yes.' Lady Clarissa scurried into the pantry and returned a minute later, holding a box. 'I hadn't unpacked it yet. I was thinking of donating it to the school, but you can use it.'

Clementine pumped her fists. 'Yes! We could have a movie night and show the film of my ballet concert too. When it's ready, of course.'

'Settle down, Clementine. You haven't even switched the thing on yet,' Aunt Violet tutted.

Basil glanced at his watch and began to collect his papers. 'I better get going. I promised Mintie I'd help her finish the concert video this evening. See you all in the morning!'

'Bye, Basil,' the group chorused as the man walked out the back door. Clementine's teacup pig, Lavender, gave a grunt and Aunt Violet's sphynx cat, Pharaoh, meowed from their basket beside the cooker.

Drew chuckled. 'Do those two always talk to the guests?'

'Lavender does,' Clementine said with a nod.

'She's cute,' Will said, glancing over at the pair.

'She's adorable,' Clementine agreed then turned back to her mother, who had begun unwrapping the camera. Clementine clapped her hands together excitedly. 'We can have the movie night in the library and use the proper projector and eat popcorn. I can help Uncle Digby make –'

'I most certainly *did* make a booking!' a woman barked in the hallway, interrupting the girl. 'It was for *this* week and it's in your *best* suite.'

Digby Pertwhistle poked his head around the kitchen door. His forehead was creased with wrinkles and his cheeks were flushed pink. 'Clarissa, may I have a quick word?'

'Of course.' Lady Clarissa stood up and hurried away.

Clementine turned the camera over in her hands, examining the buttons and dials.

A few minutes later Lady Clarissa reappeared.

'Is everything all right?' Aunt Violet asked.

'I'm afraid we have an unexpected guest.' Clarissa walked over to the reservations book, which sat on the sideboard near the telephone. She opened it but found nothing listed for that day apart from the information about the filming. 'Aunt Violet, do you remember taking a booking for a Finley Spencer?' Lady Clarissa asked. 'She said she spoke to an older woman.'

'I didn't mess up any bookings,' Aunt Violet snapped.

Clarissa sighed. 'I just wanted to know if you recalled that name.'

Aunt Violet thought for a moment. 'Actually, it does ring a bell. I had assumed that Finley Spencer was a man.'

Lady Clarissa flicked forward a week and ran her finger down the page. 'Here it is. She's booked in for next week, in the Blue Room.'

'If it helps, Will and I would be happy to move,' Drew offered. 'The Blue Room's lovely but, honestly, we're fine anywhere.'

'Are you sure?' Clarissa asked.

Drew smiled. 'Just point us in the right direction. We'll help you change the sheets and I'll wheel Will's foldaway bed into the new room.'

'Godfathers no!' Aunt Violet protested. 'Pertwhistle can change the bed.'

Drew shook his head with a chuckle. He had no doubt the old woman would have enjoyed delivering that news.

'I would like to keep Ms Spencer happy, if you and Will don't mind,' Clarissa said apologetically. With the Health and Safety Inspector due the next day, the last thing she needed was another disgruntled lodger.

'We'll go and get our things,' Drew said, standing up.

'Thank you,' Lady Clarissa replied. 'I'll take Ms Spencer through to the sitting room. Clemmie, please show Will and Drew to the Peony Suite. Aunt Violet, could you organise a fresh pot of tea for Ms Spencer?'

'Me?' the old woman grumbled. 'What do I look like – a waitress?'

Clementine giggled behind her hand and Drew gave her a wink before the three of them disappeared up the back stairs.

NOT FOR SALE

'All sorted,' Drew said as he wheeled Will's bed into the room. 'Why don't you two make a start on your movie while I give Mr Pertwhistle a hand straightening up the Blue Room?'

Uncle Digby began to protest but Drew wouldn't hear another word of it.

'Do you want to?' Clementine asked Will.

The boy looked uncertainly at his father.

Drew nodded. 'It's all right. Clementine doesn't bite.'

'Come on,' Clementine said, reaching for the boy's hand. 'We can take Lavender and Pharaoh outside. They love to chase the butterflies in the garden,' the child babbled as she led Will along the corridor and down to the kitchen. 'Lavender is really good at soccer too. Pharaoh only chases the ball a bit because he's too much of a scaredy-cat to touch it.'

Will picked up the camera and pressed a couple of buttons.

'Is it okay?' Clementine asked.

'I just had to check that it was charged properly,' he said. 'What kind of movie do you want to make?'

Clementine shrugged.

Will looked at Lavender and Pharaoh curled up in a basket by the cooker. 'They must really like each other.'

'They *love* each other,' Clementine said. 'Aunt Violet thought it was disgusting at first, but now she doesn't seem to mind.'

'We could make up a story about them,' Will suggested.

Clementine's face lit up. 'That's a great idea!'

Will grinned. 'I've never really heard of a pig and a cat in love, but Dad says that the best movies are the ones that surprise you. We should get some shots outside before the light fades too much.'

Clementine bent down to pick up Pharaoh and called to Lavender. 'You know a lot about making movies,' she said, leading the way to the garden.

'Where are you going to put Mr Doncaster tomorrow, Clarissa?' Digby Pertwhistle asked as he stirred a pot of gravy on the stove.

'I think the Sage Room might be best,' Lady Clarissa replied. 'It's quiet at the end of the hall and close to the newer bathroom.' She opened the oven to check the progress of the roast beef.

'Don't you worry about him,' Digby said. 'You run a fine establishment, and whoever made that complaint was obviously just out to cause trouble.

'Mr Doncaster's timing is terrible, with the movie being shot this week,' Clarissa said as she closed the oven door. 'The last thing we need is a bad report from the council.'

'Oh, you never know. The man might fancy being on film.' Uncle Digby chortled. 'I'm sure we could find him a part as an extra.'

Clementine was halfway down the stairs when she heard her mother and Uncle Digby talking.

'Who's Mr Doncaster?' she asked as she leapt off the bottom step and onto the flagstone floor. 'And why is the council giving us a bad report? I thought Mrs Bottomley was the only one who gave those,' the child said, referring to her Kindergarten teacher.

Lady Clarissa and Uncle Digby exchanged knowing grins. 'Mr Doncaster is the Health and Safety Inspector who is staying for a couple of days. I need you to make sure that Lavender and Pharaoh don't wander into the guest areas, and please don't leave anything lying about for anyone to trip over,' her mother instructed.

'I wonder if Mr Doncaster might not be thrilled to see a pig and a cat in the kitchen,' Uncle Digby pointed out. Although *we* know they don't go anywhere they shouldn't, *he* might not believe it.'

'Oh, heavens, I hadn't even thought of that,' Lady Clarissa said. She dreaded to think what else she'd neglected to consider.

'They can stay in my room,' Clementine offered. She picked up Pharaoh and gave him a cuddle. The sphynx nuzzled into her neck and began to purr like a lawnmower.

'I'm not sure that's a good idea, darling,' her mother replied. 'What about the back shed?'

'No, Mummy, it smells really bad,' Clementine said, wrinkling her nose.

'Who smells bad?' Aunt Violet asked, stomping down the stairs.

'The back shed,' Clementine replied.

'Old socks and dirt, it's never been any different,' Aunt Violet said with a nod. 'Why, may I ask, are we discussing that spider-infested dump?'

'Mummy wants to put Lavender and Pharaoh in there while Mr Doncaster is staying.'

'Over my dead body!' Aunt Violet barked. 'I have half a mind to put *him* in the shed.'

'That's probably not a good idea,' Uncle Digby said as he filled a large gravy boat and placed it into the oven to keep warm.

'Well, you could save yourself all this worry and just sell up to that development company that keeps pestering you, Clarissa.' Aunt Violet walked over to the dresser and counted out the knives and forks for dinner. 'You could buy yourself a lovely little cottage and never have to work again.'

Digby Pertwhistle looked up from where he was straining a saucepan of carrots. 'Where would you live then?' he asked pointedly.

The old woman curled her lip at him.

Clementine gasped. 'Sell the house? But I love our house, and Granny and Grandpa would be so sad if we left them.'

Pharaoh leapt out of the girl's arms and darted into the pantry.

'Darling, we're not going anywhere. Penberthy House is our home.' Lady Clarissa glared at the old woman. 'Why don't you help Aunt Violet set the table?'

Clementine washed her hands and counted out the placemats. 'I asked Will if he wanted to have dinner with us in the kitchen but he said he'd rather be with his dad,' she said with a tinge of disappointment.

'I think Will's a bit shy, darling. It's probably for the best that Ms Spencer has some company tonight, and there's plenty of time for the two of you to play during the rest of the week,' her mother replied.

'We're not playing, Mummy,' Clementine said. 'We're making a proper movie, and Pharaoh and Lavender are the stars.'

'Speaking of which, we still haven't solved the problem of what to do with our little friends for the next few days,' Uncle Digby said as he finished plating up three roast dinners for their guests. 'What about the boarding kennel and cattery over in Highton Mill?'

'No!' Clementine gasped. 'Please don't take them away.'

'No, indeed!' Aunt Violet huffed. 'I won't have my boy cavorting with the local riffraff.'

Clementine thought hard. 'Tilda and Teddy could look after them, and then Flash could be in our movie too,' she said excitedly.

'I still don't see why they have to go any-where.' Aunt Violet pursed her lips. 'If that man doesn't like how we live, too bad.'

Lady Clarissa took off her apron and picked up two of the plates. Digby Pertwhistle took the third and balanced the gravy boat on a silver tray.

'I don't think we can afford to take that chance, Aunt Violet,' Lady Clarissa said as she and Uncle Digby headed for the door. 'I'll give Ana a call after dinner.'

Lavender walked over to Clementine and looked up at the girl. The little pig seemed to know something was up.

Clementine leaned down to give her a scratch. 'I think you might be having a sleepover with Flash and Pharaoh. It will be lots of fun, just like when Tilda and Teddy stay here.'

'Don't be silly, Clementine,' Aunt Violet said. 'Pharaoh won't have any fun while he's away. He'll miss me far too much.'

Clementine opened her mouth to say something but decided she'd better not. It was probably best Aunt Violet didn't know that Pharaoh had howled all day when Mrs Mogg had told the cat Aunt Violet was on her way to pick him up after their holiday by the sea.

AACHOO!

'How's everything going in there?' Lady Clarissa asked as Uncle Digby returned with a tray of empty plates.

'They seem to be having a lovely time,' the man replied. 'Ms Spencer is charming and she's been hooting at Drew's stories all night.'

'Oh, that's a relief.' Lady Clarissa smiled. 'Dessert's almost ready.'

The woman loaded the silver tray with three bowls of home-made apple pie and ice-cream for Uncle Digby to take to the guests.

Clementine picked up her plate and walked over to the sink.

Lady Clarissa glanced across the bench just as Uncle Digby disappeared through the swinging kitchen door. 'Oh, silly me. I forgot the cream.'

'I can take it, Mummy,' Clementine offered.

'Are you sure you can manage it?' Clarissa asked, handing her the crystal jug.

The child nodded. 'I'll be careful.'

Clementine gripped the handle with one hand and rested her other hand beneath it. Her mother held open the door and Clementine walked into the hallway. She was halfway to the dining room when her nose began to itch.

'Stop it,' the child said to her nose, but the sneeze refused to wait. Clementine looked around for somewhere to put the jug. She was too far from the front hall table, so she quickly set it on the floor and dived into her pocket for a tissue.

'Aachoo!'

Clementine sneezed twice more before the tickle stopped. She carefully wiped her nose and put the tissue back into her pocket, then turned around to retrieve the jug.

'Pharaoh! No!' she exclaimed.

Upon hearing his name, the cat lifted his head. A dribble of cream wobbled on his chin.

'Is everything all right, Clementine?' Uncle Digby asked, appearing in the hallway.

The child spun around while Pharaoh slunk away. 'I was bringing the cream but then I felt a sneeze and I didn't want it to go in the jug, so I put it down,' she began to explain.

'Good girl. I was just on my way to fetch some for Ms Spencer.' The man picked up the jug and hurried away before Clementine had time to finish.

'But . . .' Clementine gulped and rushed after him.

By the time she reached the dining room, the jug had been placed in the middle of the table. Clementine spotted Will and waved. He grinned and waved back.

The girl turned to Ms Spencer, who was sitting opposite Drew and Will. 'Hello,

I'm Clementine,' she said brightly, keeping one eye on the jug.

Digby turned around, wondering why Clementine had followed him in.

'Oh, hello,' the lady replied. The woman's honey-coloured hair fell over her shoulders in loose curls and she wore a teal silk blouse with a ruffle at the front.

Clemmie's eyes wandered to the lady's hand. 'That ring is ginormous,' she blurted out.

'It's an emerald.' Ms Spencer fanned out her fingers for Clementine to get a closer look.

'Are you staying for long?' Clementine asked.

'For as long as I need to,' the woman replied mysteriously.

Digby Pertwhistle walked over to Clementine and began ushering her from the room. 'We should be getting back to the kitchen,' he said. 'I'm sure our guests would like to eat their dessert in peace.'

'See you tomorrow, Clemmie,' Will said, waving his spoon in the air.

Clementine hesitated, unsure of what to do. It wouldn't be right to serve the cream to the guests. As she watched Ms Spencer reach across the table for the jug, Clementine's heart thumped. 'I'll get it!' she yelped, diving for it.

Their hands collided, sending the crystal pitcher flying. Cream splashed down the table and all over Ms Spencer.

'What did you do that for?' the woman cried out. Her beautiful silk blouse now resembled a preschooler's spatter painting.

'I'm s-s-sorry,' Clementine stammered. 'I just wanted to help.'

Digby Pertwhistle rushed in to set the jug upright and stem the tide of cream. 'Oh, I'm terribly sorry.'

Finley Spencer dabbed at the white splodges with her napkin.

Will, looking as if he'd swallowed a fly, watched on in horrified silence.

'It's just a bit of cream,' Drew whispered to Clementine. 'Accidents happen.'

'Not to me, they don't,' Finley Spencer barked.

'Clemmie, please run and get a cloth from the kitchen,' Digby Pertwhistle instructed the child.

Clementine looked at Ms Spencer. 'I didn't mean to,' she whispered before dashing from the room.

'Ms Spencer, we'll have your blouse dry-cleaned in the morning,' Digby said.

'Yes, you will,' the woman snapped.

Clementine charged through the kitchen door, leaving it swinging wildly in her wake.

Her mother looked up from the table, where she had just poured two cups of tea for herself and Aunt Violet. 'What's the matter, darling?'

'I spilled the cream,' Clementine said. 'But I had to.'

'Oh dear.' Lady Clarissa jumped up and grabbed some cloths from the sideboard. 'Stay here. You can tell me what happened when I get back.'

Her mother darted from the room.

'What do you mean you had to?' Aunt Violet asked.

Clementine took a deep breath. 'I was taking the cream and I sneezed and –'

Aunt Violet shook her head. 'Godfathers, Clementine, why didn't you just bring it back and change it over? You can't serve cream with snot in it.'

'It didn't have snot in it,' Clementine said. 'I put the cream down so I could sneeze, but then Pharaoh licked it.'

'Oh.' Aunt Violet pulled a face.

'Uncle Digby took it before I could tell him what happened,' Clementine said. 'I couldn't let Ms Spencer eat cream with cat spit in it, so I tried to pick it up but then we knocked it over and now it's everywhere.'

'Never mind, Clementine,' Aunt Violet said. She could feel a headache coming on.

'Ms Spencer was really, really angry. I just didn't want Mummy to get a bad report from the council.' Clementine's eyes began filling with tears.

'Your mother won't be getting any bad reports,' Aunt Violet said. 'The man from the council isn't here until tomorrow, and I'm sure Ms Spencer knows it was just an accident. It would have been much worse if you'd served her the cream. Although, you could have stayed quiet and no one would have been any the wiser.'

Clementine recoiled at such an idea.

'Don't look at me like that,' Aunt Violet said. 'I was joking. Come here.'

Clementine walked around to her great-aunt, who wrapped her arms around the child. Clementine leaned in and put her head on Aunt Violet's shoulder.

'Why don't I take you upstairs and run your bath?' the old woman suggested. 'You can practise your lines tomorrow.'

Clementine sniffed. She looked up at Aunt Violet and nodded. 'Yes, please.'

ALFIE DONCASTER

'Ow are you feeling this morning, Clementine?' Lady Clarissa asked as she helped the child wriggle into a beautiful white drop-waisted dress with a wide grey bow.

Clementine's big blue eyes widened as she looked at her mother. 'I'm sorry about what happened, Mummy.'

'Clemmie, it was just a misunderstanding. I know you were trying to do the right thing,' her mother said. 'Next time, though, it might be better to ask one of us for help rather than covering the guests in cream.'

Clementine gave a little grin. 'Is Ms Spencer still angry?'

Lady Clarissa shook her head and smiled. 'Uncle Digby's taking her blouse to be cleaned this morning and I offered her a special afternoon tea. I'm sure she's already forgotten about it all.'

'Aunt Violet was really kind to me last night,' Clementine said. 'She's a lot nicer than when she first came.'

Her mother nodded. 'Yes, sometimes I think she's almost the same person I knew when I was a little girl.'

'Before she got barnacles?' Clementine said, remembering the way her mother had described the woman when she'd received that fateful letter announcing Aunt Violet's impending arrival.

'Yes,' Lady Clarissa giggled, 'before she got barnacles.'

Digby Pertwhistle knocked on Clementine's bedroom door and poked his head around.

'Good morning, Clementine,' the man said. 'Don't you look lovely.'

'Thank you, Uncle Digby,' Clementine said as her mother pinned back her hair with a large white bow.

'Clarissa, our guests have all finished their breakfast, and Drew and Basil are setting up in the library,' the man said. 'Ms Spencer has gone up to her room, although I have given her a few brochures for some of the local attractions. I thought she might like to go out for a while.'

'Wonderful. We'll be down in a jiffy,' Lady Clarissa said before Digby left them.

'I wish Lavender and Pharaoh didn't have to go,' Clementine said sadly. Ana Hobbs had called in early that morning to pick up her two house guests while Clementine and her mother had been eating breakfast. 'Can you take me to see them this afternoon?'

'I'm not sure if I'll have time, Clemmie. Perhaps Aunt Violet will go for a walk with you,' Lady Clarissa replied.

Clementine nodded and decided she'd ask her straight away.

Lady Clarissa was returning Clementine's hairbrush to the dressing table when she spied something jutting out from under the bed. 'Darling, what's that?'

Clementine pulled out a dark timber chest a little bit bigger than a shoebox. 'I found it in the attic when we were cleaning up for the fete, but there isn't a key. You said that I could keep it, remember?'

Lady Clarissa took it from Clementine and sat it on the bed. It was a pretty thing, with an inlaid geometrical carving in a lighter-coloured timber on top. 'Oh, yes,' she said, tracing her finger over the pattern.

'If only we could open it,' Clementine sighed.

'I found a whole box of keys when I was looking for photographs the other week,' Lady Clarissa said. 'I'll get them later and we can see if any of them work.'

'Maybe there's some treasure inside, like when we found Granny's jewels and Flash,'

Clementine gasped. Tilda and Teddy's tortoise had once gone missing, only to be located in an old jewellery box at the fair.

'Oh, I hope there aren't any animals in there – I don't think they'd be in a very good way by now. You never know, there might be something interesting,' her mother agreed. 'Anyway, we'd better get a move on.'

Clementine slipped her hand into her mother's and the pair hurried downstairs.

Clementine was on her way to the toilet when the front doorbell rang.

'I'll get it,' she called out as she opened the door.

A short man in a camel-coloured suit stood on the porch. He wore a white shirt with a brown-and-yellow striped tie and was carrying a tan briefcase in one hand and a small suitcase in the other. He had a funny pork-pie hat on his head with tufts of grey hair poking out at the sides.

'Hello,' the child said. 'May I help you?'

The man looked Clementine up and down, wondering if she was always dressed as though she were living in the 1800s.

Clementine realised that he was staring at her with an odd expression. 'Basil is making a film and I'm my great-great granny today,' she explained. 'But I'm really Clementine.'

'I see.' The man nodded. 'My name is Alfie Doncaster and –'

Clementine inhaled sharply. 'The man with the bad reports,' she whispered.

A row of lines knitted across his brow.

Clementine gulped. 'Come in,' she said, remembering her manners. 'I'll get Mummy.'

The child turned and scurried down the hall to the library, leaving Mr Doncaster on his own.

'People only get bad reports if they deserve them,' Alfie muttered to himself. 'I'm not the big, bad wolf, you know.'

He set his bags on the floor and surveyed the entrance hall, making a mental note of the

room. The wide floorboards gleamed as did every other piece of furniture in sight. Alfie pulled a small contraption from his coat pocket and held it against an enormous mirror, which hung above an antique side table. He waited a moment then read the numbers on the screen before checking his reflection. Then he straightened his hat and turned around, just in time to see a pretty woman striding towards him.

'Good afternoon, Mr Doncaster. I'm Clarissa Appleby.' The woman smiled and held out her hand, glancing warily at the device he was holding.

'Yes, hello.' Alfie shook her hand warmly. 'Lovely to meet you, Lady Appleby.'

'Please, call me Clarissa,' the woman replied. 'May I ask what that is?'

'Oh, this is my shine-o-meter, and I am pleased to say that your mirror has an almost-perfect sheen.'

Clarissa exhaled gently. 'Would you like to go straight to your room, Mr Doncaster? You can leave your suitcase here. The butler will bring it up shortly.'

'If I may, I'd like to get started as soon as possible, and no need for anyone else to carry my bags,' the man said. 'I can manage.'

'Of course. Please follow me.' Clarissa beckoned and started up the stairs.

Her heart was pounding and she felt as if she'd swallowed a handful of sand, but there was no way she was going to let Mr Doncaster see her nerves.

'I'm afraid you've come at an interesting time, Mr Doncaster.' Lady Clarissa turned and smiled at him as they reached the first-floor landing. 'We're actually in the throes of filming a documentary. I hadn't planned on any guests this week at all.'

'A documentary, you say?'

'Yes, Basil Hobbs is directing. He's making a feature film on stately homes,' Clarissa replied, 'and ours is one of them.'

'I love his work. I took Mrs Doncaster to see that last movie he made on the castles of France and we both thought it was marvellous.'

'Mr Doncaster, is it possible to know the exact nature of your enquiries here?' Lady Clarissa asked as tactfully as she dared.

The man looked at her. 'I wish I could tell you – I really do – but guests rely on their anonymity. Lady Appleby, from what I've seen so far, I suspect you have nothing to worry about.'

The woman sighed. 'That is a relief. I can assure you, Mr Doncaster, we pride ourselves on having very high standards.'

'We shall get along just fine then,' Alfie said as they came to a stop outside a doorway at the end of the hall.

'This is the Sage Room.' Clarissa turned the key in the lock and pushed open the door, promptly pulling it closed again at lightning speed. She spun around, praying the man hadn't seen a thing. 'I'm terribly sorry but I've made a mistake. You're not in this room at all. Silly me.'

Alfie Doncaster frowned. 'Is everything all right, Lady Appleby?'

'Yes, yes, I think the butler must have taken a last-minute booking while I was busy this morning. If you wouldn't mind coming back to the sitting room, I'll arrange tea and scones while I sort out a room for you,' Clarissa babbled. She could feel a red flush creeping up her neck.

'Well, I would like to get started soon,' Mr Doncaster said, 'but I have driven quite a long way and a cup of tea would be nice.'

Lady Clarissa directed the man to the sitting room, where everything seemed to be in order. 'Please excuse me. I won't be a minute.'

The woman rushed away to the kitchen, where she was relieved to find Digby Pertwhistle unpacking the groceries.

'Hello Clarissa. How's the shoot going?' the man asked.

'Uncle Digby, have you been in the Sage Room?' she asked, catching her breath.

'Not since I checked it last night. Whatever's the matter?'

Lady Clarissa bit her lip. 'It's a disaster.'

'A disaster?' Digby frowned. It wasn't like Clarissa to be so flustered.

'Yes, the bed is unmade and there are toys strewn from one end of it to the other. I've got to run back and sort it out, and I'll have to find another room for Mr Doncaster. Would you mind arranging tea and scones for him? Mr Doncaster's in the sitting room. Thank heavens I didn't just give him the key.'

Digby Pertwhistle shot over to the sink and filled the kettle. 'I'm sure that room was perfect when I left it last night.' He wondered if he was losing his marbles, particularly as he'd mislaid his master key too. It was most unlike him.

Clementine skipped into the kitchen. 'Hello Mummy. Basil said that I could have something to eat because I got my scene right in just two takes.' The child held out two fingers on her right hand. 'Aunt Violet and the others will be here soon for morning tea too.'

'Clementine, have you been in the Sage Room?' her mother asked sharply.

The child shook her head.

Lady Clarissa's lips formed a tight line as she considered her daughter.

'Excuse me, Clarissa, but should I also make tea for Ms Spencer?' Digby asked.

'She's gone out,' Clementine piped up. 'I saw her at the front door. I was glad she didn't see me in case she's still mad about last night.'

'Just make enough for one,' Lady Clarissa said to Digby. 'I'll be back in a bit and then, young lady –' she turned to Clementine – 'you and I need to talk.'

The woman rushed up the back stairs, leaving Clementine to ponder what was the matter.

'I'll get you something in a few minutes, Clemmie,' Uncle Digby said as he arranged two plump scones on a plate with a pot of cream and another of home-made raspberry jam, and disappeared out the door.

MYSTERIOUS MESSES

Clementine's tummy gurgled, and she looked around the kitchen for something to eat.

Several scones sat under the glass dome on the bench and there was a big white box next to it. She lifted the lid and peered inside at a delicious-looking strawberry sponge cake.

'Yum!' Clementine licked her lips. She loved Pierre's sponge cakes almost as much as Uncle Digby loved Pierre's cream buns. Clementine glanced at the empty basket beside the cooker, thinking how sad Lavender and Pharaoh would be about missing out on the cake.

She wondered what was taking everyone so long when, suddenly, she had a bright idea. She would organise the morning tea herself! It couldn't be that difficult and, besides, she was almost six years old.

Clementine stood in front of the dresser on her tippy toes and reached as high as she could. Her fingertips touched the bottom of the plate rack but she couldn't quite get there. She pulled a chair over from the kitchen table and clambered onto it, carefully pulling down one plate at a time and stacking them on the dresser top. Then she counted out the cups and saucers and, finally, the cutlery.

A few minutes later, Clementine surveyed the neatly laid table. There was something missing.

'Napkins!' she exclaimed, and hurried into the pantry.

Clementine knew which ones she was after. They were blue and white and were her mother's favourites. She searched high and low when at last she heard footsteps in the kitchen.

'I'm in here, Uncle Digby,' she called out, hoping he would be able to point her in the right direction. Instead, Clementine heard a dull thud. She shrugged, not thinking anything of it. Penberthy House made lots of noises.

When Clementine was just about to give up and settle on a set of rose-coloured napkins, she caught sight of the blue-and-white ones underneath.

'Godfathers! What on earth's happened in here?' Clementine heard Aunt Violet shout.

The child emerged with a handful of the pretty linen serviettes. 'Hello Aunt Violet, I was just setting the table for morning tea and I almost forgot the napkins. I know that you don't like it when they're missing, so I –'

'No, I meant that! There!' The old woman pointed at Pierre's strawberry sponge cake, which appeared to have exploded on the flag-stone floor with the box collapsed around it.

Clementine clapped her hand over her mouth, dropping the napkins. 'But it was on the bench.'

'It's certainly not there now,' Aunt Violet said, folding her arms. 'I suppose it magically leapt off all by itself?'

Clementine shrugged. 'I don't know.'

'Well, Mr Doncaster seems like a perfectly nice human being,' Uncle Digby declared as he walked in from the hallway. 'Oh dear,' he said, spotting the mess. 'What happened?'

At that moment, Lady Clarissa arrived down the back stairs and immediately spied the cake catastrophe. 'Oh my goodness! Not another disaster.'

'I wanted to surprise you, Mummy,' Clementine started to explain.

'You've certainly achieved that,' Aunt Violet said.

Lady Clarissa turned to her daughter. 'This is not a very good surprise, Clementine, especially after what I found in the Sage Room. When were you playing in there? I told you not to leave anything lying about.'

'But I haven't been in there,' the child said.

'I found these.' Her mother held up a skipping rope and a long rubber python. 'I've just thrown a whole heap more of your things back into your room.'

'But I put them away.' Clementine could feel her eyes pricking.

'And you shouldn't have tried to move that cake on your own,' her mother admonished. 'It's far too big.'

'I didn't move the cake,' Clementine protested. 'I was in the pantry getting the napkins and I heard someone in the kitchen. They must have done it.'

Lady Clarissa frowned. 'Clementine, you know how important it is to tell the truth,' she said.

'But I am.' The child's bottom lip began to tremble and fat tears wobbled in the corners of her eyes. She looked to Uncle Digby and Aunt Violet for support, only to find the same look of disappointment on their faces.

'Oh, darling, please don't cry. Why don't you take these things up to your room and wash your face?' Lady Clarissa suggested. 'We can talk about it when you come back down.'

Clementine sniffed and brushed at the tears that refused to stop. She picked up the skipping rope and rubber snake and raced up the back stairs, wishing Lavender was home.

'I wonder if we might be able to rescue some of this cake.' Uncle Digby bent down to inspect the damage. The centre of it was still sitting on the base of the white box. 'I made some jelly this morning. Perhaps I could fashion a trifle for morning tea.'

'Ugh, *I'm* not eating it!' Aunt Violet shuddered.

Uncle Digby grabbed a spatula and a large plate and knelt down on the floor. Just as he was about to lever the flattened cake out of the mangled box there was a knock on the kitchen door. Mr Doncaster poked his head in.

'Hello,' he called in a singsong voice.

Digby Pertwhistle froze.

Lady Clarissa spun around and tugged gently on her skirt, trying to obscure Mr Doncaster's view.

But it was Aunt Violet who saved the day. She glided over to the fellow and stood directly in front of him. 'Hello,' she purred. 'I'm Violet Appleby and you must be Mr Doncaster.'

'Yes, I just wanted to let Mr Pertwhistle know that they were the most delicious scones I've ever eaten,' the man said. He patted his round tummy. 'I'm a bit of a connoisseur.'

'Well, why don't I bring you some more?' Aunt Violet took Mr Doncaster by the arm and steered him back into the hallway.

MYSTERIES

Clementine shot up the back stairs, her face blotchy and wet with tears.

'Um, hello,' a small voice called out.

Clementine looked up to see Will standing in the hallway. She blinked her big blue eyes but her lip refused to stop trembling.

Will pulled out a tissue from his pocket and offered it to the girl. 'What's wrong?'

'Mummy thinks I left my toys in the Sage Room and that I dropped the cake, but I didn't,' Clementine blurted.

Will frowned, puzzled. His father walked up behind him and stopped. 'Clementine, what's wrong?' the man asked gently.

'I didn't do it and Mummy thinks that I did,' Clementine sobbed. 'Mr Doncaster will give us a bad report and Mummy will have to sell the house and we won't have anywhere to live.' She could barely speak for the hiccupy gulps.

'I can't believe anyone would ever give your mother a bad report,' Drew said with a smile. 'The woman's an angel.'

Clementine blew her nose and wiped her eyes. 'I try my best to tell the truth. I really do.'

'I'm sure you do.' Drew grinned.

'I have to take my things upstairs,' Clementine said, remembering the skipping rope and rubber snake in her hand.

'Would you like some help?' Will asked. Drew smiled at the boy.

Clementine nodded. Will offered her his hand and the two of them walked upstairs to the third floor. Clementine opened her bedroom door.

'What a mess!' she exclaimed, turning to Will. 'It's not usually like this.'

Her mother must have been very cross because it looked as if she'd stood at the door and thrown everything inside. In the middle of the floor lay a doll with her right arm sticking straight up next to her head and her left leg kinked at an awkward angle.

Clementine bent down to pick her up and gasped. 'It's Nellie! I didn't recognise her.' She stared into the doll's glassy eyes. 'Her hair is all chopped off.'

'Whoever did it mustn't like dolls very much,' Will said, examining the shaggy crop. 'She looks like she's been attacked by a hedge trimmer.'

A giggle escaped from Clementine's lips, and Will grinned at her.

'Thanks,' Clementine said.

'What for?'

'Being my friend.'

Will blushed. 'I don't have a lot of friends.'

'Why?' Clementine asked.

'I don't like talking to people very much,' the boy replied. 'Not since Mum went away.'

Clementine frowned. 'Where did she go?'

'Heaven. Is that where your dad is too?'

Clementine looked surprised. 'I don't know where he is. Uncle Digby found me in a basket of dinner rolls in the back of Pierre's van.'

'What do you mean Uncle Digby found you?' Will wondered if he'd heard her properly.

'Mummy adopted me,' Clementine said.

'Don't you want to know who your real mum and dad are?' Will asked.

Clementine shook her head. 'Mummy's my real mummy now. She loves me and so does Uncle Digby. Even Aunt Violet loves me when she's not being mean.' She paused for a moment. 'You have a great dad.'

Will nodded. 'Your mum's nice. My dad thinks so too.'

For a moment neither of the children said a thing.

Clementine sighed. 'I wish I could find out who was in the kitchen. Do you think the person who dropped the cake is the same person who put my toys in the Sage Room? I know I didn't leave them there.'

'Maybe we should look for clues to see who did it,' Will suggested.

Clementine's eyes widened. 'That's a great idea,' she said, opening the lid of her giant toy box. 'We can be detectives, like on the television. Except I don't know how to take fingerprints and I haven't got one of those giant spyglass things.'

'It's okay. You don't need all that stuff to be a detective,' Will said.

Together, he and Clementine began to put everything away. Along with the doll there was a scruffy old bear, a jigsaw puzzle and some building blocks.

Clementine picked up her skipping rope and rubber python and dumped them into the toy box. She was just about to close it when she felt something under the lid. Clementine peered underneath and saw a tiny paper envelope taped inside.

'Look at this,' she said to Will.

The boy stretched his neck to see.

Clementine tried to pull it free but it was stuck tight. She pushed the lid the whole way up and leaned it against the wall. The envelope was sealed but there was clearly something inside. Clementine pressed her fingers against the paper.

'What's in it?' Will asked.

'It feels like a key,' Clementine said.

Will looked around to see if there was anything they could use to prise it free. He spotted a pair of scissors on Clementine's desk and promptly ran to get them.

After pushing and prodding, the yellowed envelope fell on top of the rubber snake. Clementine picked it up. The paper was old but it was tough. Will cut the end off and shook a small brass key into his palm.

'What do you think it's for?' he asked.

Clementine looked at the lock on her toy box. 'It's too small for this,' she said with a shrug, and shut the lid.

Will handed her the key and she carefully placed it in her pocket.

'But maybe . . .' Clementine looked over at the little wooden box she'd pulled out from under her bed that morning.

Will read her mind, and the two children rushed over to it.

'We *are* like detectives.' Clementine grinned. Her heart began to beat faster as she pulled the key out and pushed it into the lock.

Click.

'It fits!' Will exclaimed. 'Go on, open it.'

Clementine turned the key and the lock sprung apart. She pushed the lid up and, holding their breaths, she and Will peered inside.

Clementine and Will charged downstairs into the kitchen, which was abuzz with chatter.

Basil, Drew and Aunt Violet were sitting around the table and Uncle Digby was serving tea from the pot.

'Where's Mummy?' Clementine jigged about impatiently, clutching the little timber box.

'You look a lot happier than before,' Drew remarked.

'Your mother's taken Mr Doncaster up to his room but she should be back any minute,' Uncle Digby replied.

Clementine placed the box on the table and climbed up onto a chair. Will sat on the seat beside her.

'What have you got there, Clementine?' Basil asked.

'I found this in the attic a while ago and Mummy said I could keep it in my room because it's so pretty,' Clementine babbled excitedly. 'Will and I just found the key.'

'How marvellous!' Basil enthused. 'Can you show us what's inside?'

'When Mummy comes back,' Clementine said firmly. She was bursting to show everyone what they had found but she wanted her mother to see it first.

'In the meantime, can I offer anyone more trifle?' Uncle Digby asked. A large bowl of cake and jelly was sitting on the bench.

Drew picked up his empty bowl. 'Well, if there's some left over, I'd hate to see it go to waste.'

'What about you, Clemmie? Will?' Uncle Digby asked as he filled Drew's dish.

'No, thank you, Uncle Digby,' Clementine replied. 'But not because it was on the floor.'

Aunt Violet arched an eyebrow. 'I'd keep quiet about that if I were you.'

Lady Clarissa walked through from the hallway.

'Is Mr Doncaster happy with his room?' Uncle Digby asked.

'Yes, I think so,' Clarissa replied. 'He does seem like a very nice man. I hope I was worried about nothing.'

'I'm sure you were,' Drew said. 'I can't imagine what he'd find fault with. You're perfect.'

The adults stopped talking and looked at one another with wry smiles. Lady Clarissa's cheeks reddened.

'What I meant is that you're a perfect hostess and the house is beautiful.' Drew's neck seemed to be turning a dark shade of crimson.

'Thank you.' Clarissa bit her lip. 'I just hope there are no other mishaps.' She walked up behind Clementine and gave the girl a hug, whispering into her ear.

Clementine looked back at her. 'I love you too, Mummy, and I promise I didn't do those things.'

Lady Clarissa nodded. It wasn't like Clementine to tell lies. There had to be another explanation, though she wasn't yet sure what it might be.

The woman noticed the box on the table. 'Darling, I won't have time to go through the keys just now. I'm taking Mr Doncaster on a tour of the house in ten minutes.'

'But we *found* the key, Mummy,' Clementine exclaimed, 'and we know what's inside.'

'Oh, really?' Clementine's mother leaned over the child's shoulder, eager to see the box's mysterious contents.

Clementine lifted the lid. 'It's photographs.' She turned around and looked at her mother excitedly. 'And there's one of me.'

'That's a surprise. I thought I knew where all of the family pictures were,' Clarissa said, glancing quickly at the picture Clementine was holding before she picked up a bundle. The one on top was of a baby in a christening gown. She turned it over and smiled.

'Don't keep us in suspense, Clarissa,' Aunt Violet demanded. 'Who is it?'

'Remember when you said there were no photographs of you as a child? I think you might be wrong about that.' Lady Clarissa held up the picture for everyone to see.

'Brilliant!' Basil clapped his hands.

Aunt Violet pursed her lips. 'Really! Well, that is a surprise.'

The first part of the pile were all shots of Aunt Violet as a baby and toddler. Lady Clarissa flipped through them before she passed them to her aunt, who cringed with false modesty.

Clementine pulled out another photograph. 'Look, Mummy. There's another one of me.'

Lady Clarissa frowned.

Clementine studied the picture more closely. 'But that's not Lavender. That's a dog. I don't have a dog.'

'May I see that, please?' Aunt Violet reached across the table. Her face softened into a smile. 'Clementine, that's not you. It's me and my Paisley. He was a West Highland Terrier and I loved him to bits.'

The girl's eyes grew round in astonishment. 'We look like twins, Aunt Violet,' she said.

'Heavens. It's uncanny.' Aunt Violet's eyebrows knotted as she studied the picture.

'Goodness, look at the time.' Lady Clarissa took the photograph from her aunt's hand, returned it to the box and snapped the lid shut. 'I think you lot had better get back to the library or poor Ana and the children won't have you home before dark, Basil.'

Drew wondered at the hasty end to Clementine's discovery.

'Where do you think you're going with those?' Aunt Violet demanded. 'I believe they belong to me.'

'I thought you and I could go through them later to see if there's anything Basil might be able to use for the film,' Lady Clarissa explained. 'I need you to look after Clemmie on set while I take Mr Doncaster through the house.'

Clarissa passed the box to Uncle Digby and whispered something. The man nodded and promptly disappeared.

'Well, if that was morning tea, it appears we've had it,' Aunt Violet said, rising from her chair. 'Come along, Clementine. I'll fix your hair and see if we can't straighten that dress up a bit.' Clementine's drop-waisted bow was looking a bit worse for wear.

'Will you listen to my lines?' Clementine asked.

'Of course.' The old woman hesitated for a second and looked at Clementine.

'What's wrong, Aunt Violet?' the child asked.

'Nothing,' Aunt Violet said, shaking her head. 'Nothing at all.'

Moments later the kitchen was empty.

HOUSEKEEPING

'Are you happy in the Marigold Room, Mr Doncaster?' Lady Clarissa enquired as she met the man in the front hall.

'Yes, it's very comfortable, thank you,' Alfie replied, clutching his briefcase in his left hand. 'Now, where shall we start?'

'Please follow me.' Lady Clarissa smiled at him nervously, wondering about the contents of his briefcase. She had decided it was best to begin from the bottom and work their way up.

They would start with the sitting room then move to the dining room and the music room, before ending up in the library once filming had finished for the day.

Clarissa pushed open the double doors to the sitting room and led the way inside.

'This is a lovely room,' Mr Doncaster said, admiring the plump floral couches and grand fireplace with its sandstone surround. 'I imagine much of the furniture is original.'

'Yes, that little table –' Clarissa pointed at a very pretty piece – 'was a wedding gift to my grandparents from King Frederick, Queen Georgiana's father.'

'How fascinating.' Alfie Doncaster sat his briefcase on the floor and took a pair of white gloves from his jacket pocket. He pulled them on and then ran a forefinger along the table.

The woman watched as he held up his hand and inspected the tip of the glove.

'A promising start,' Mr Doncaster declared.

He proceeded to the mantelpiece and did the same, then worked his way around the room, checking every hard surface, including the windowsills and skirting boards.

'I must say, Lady Clarissa,' Mr Doncaster said, studying the glove closely, 'I can't see a speck of dust and that is no mean feat given the age of this place.'

He then produced his shine-o-meter and ran it over the timber furniture, smiling at the result.

Clarissa exhaled with relief. She watched with fascination as the man pulled a small hand-held vacuum from his briefcase and unscrewed the telescopic handle.

He pressed a switch and the motor whirred to life. Once again Mr Doncaster walked around the room, this time vacuuming the lounges and curtains and several spots on the carpet. When he was satisfied that he'd taken enough care with his samples, he pulled the contraption apart and examined the filter inside.

The man gave her a nod of approval. 'Congratulations, Lady Clarissa, I'm very impressed.'

He set down the vacuum and took out a clipboard, on which he wrote several notes.

'Well, I think we're finished in here,' Mr Doncaster said. 'Where are we off to next?'

'The dining room. It's just across the hall,' Lady Clarissa said, turning to lead the way.

Mr Doncaster's eyes were everywhere as they continued the tour. Clarissa opened the dining-room door and, just as she did, a terrible smell invaded her nostrils. She couldn't possibly pull another door shut on the man's face but she had to do something. Her mind raced.

'Actually, Mr Doncaster, it might be better to go to the music room first,' she said, trying not to sound desperate. 'I think today's filming will be over earlier than Basil had first anticipated, so we could go straight from the music room to the library next door.'

'No, no, we're here now, so let's get on with it.' The man barged past her. 'And don't look so nervous, Lady Clarissa. From what I see you've got nothing to – oh, pooh! What's that awful smell?'

Lady Clarissa rushed after him. 'I have no idea,' she gulped.

'Well, we must find the source immediately,' the man said dramatically. He placed his briefcase on the sideboard and flicked the locks, pulling out a disposable face mask. He then put on a fresh pair of rubber gloves.

'Would you like a mask and gloves, Lady Clarissa?' he mumbled through the covering. 'I have spares.'

Clarissa shook her head, mystified.

'Suit yourself.' Alfie Doncaster walked around the room, checking all surfaces. He then knelt down and lifted the mask up onto his forehead. Lady Clarissa was horrified when he began sniffing the carpet.

'Mr Doncaster, I can assure you, our carpets are steam-cleaned every three months – and sometimes more often if they need it,' she said.

But the man was like a bloodhound, down on all-fours with his tail in the air.

Just as Alfie's bottom was poking out from under the dining-room table, Aunt Violet and Clementine walked into the room.

'Excuse me, Clarissa,' Aunt Violet began. 'Godfathers, what's that ghastly smell? And what's he doing under there?'

Lady Clarissa's whole body tensed. She began waving wildly at her aunt and daughter, hoping they would get the message and leave.

'We've finished for today, Mummy,' Clementine said, pinching her nose. 'Can Drew take me and Will to see Lavender and Pharaoh, please? We want to make some more of our movie.'

'It's "Will and I", Clementine,' Aunt Violet corrected the girl. 'Will and I.'

Clementine sighed. 'Sorry, Aunt Violet.'

Lady Clarissa nodded. 'Yes, run along while I help Mr Doncaster with this little problem.'

'Check under the sideboard,' Aunt Violet whispered. 'I saw Lavender making her way out of here early this morning before breakfast.'

'Lavender wouldn't poo on the carpet, Aunt Violet!' Clementine said loudly.

At the mention of poo, Alfie Doncaster's ears pricked up. He raised his head too quickly and bashed it on the underside of the table as

he backed out. 'Ow!' he complained, rubbing his crown.

'Are you all right, Mr Doncaster?' Lady Clarissa rushed to him, shooing Aunt Violet and Clementine from the room with a flutter of her hand.

'Who's Lavender?' Mr Doncaster asked.

'She's my teacup piggy,' Clementine said.

'A pig, you say? Do you mean a toy pig?' Mr Doncaster asked, his left eyebrow rising so high it looked as if it were about to fly right off the top of his forehead.

Clementine shook her head. 'Lavender's real. She's just miniature, that's all.'

'And where is she now?' Mr Doncaster asked, glaring at Lady Clarissa.

The woman cleared her throat and was about to say something when Clementine jumped in. 'She and Pharaoh are having a sleepover with Flash at Basil and Ana's.'

Lady Clarissa gave her daughter a deflated look.

'Just until you . . .' Clementine saw her mother's face and clamped her hand over her mouth, but it was too late.

'Clemmie, you don't want to keep Drew and Will waiting, do you?' Lady Clarissa said, willing Clementine to leave before she said anything else that could ruin them.

'No, I think you should stay right here, Clementine,' Alfie Doncaster said. 'You're a very honest little girl.'

Clementine swallowed hard and gave a small nod.

The man sniffed the air. His nose led him to the sideboard, where he quickly got down on all-fours again and stuck his head under the piece of furniture. 'I have found the source of the offending smell,' he announced.

Clementine bent down to take a look. 'It's a poo,' she said, wrinkling her nose.

Alfie Doncaster whipped what appeared to be a retractable pooper scooper from his back pocket and nimbly removed the smelly surprise.

Clementine shook her head. 'That's not a pig poo. It's much too big. It looks like one of Pharaoh's.'

Lady Clarissa pressed the heel of her palm against her forehead.

'I presume Pharaoh is a dog,' Mr Doncaster said. He popped the poop into a little plastic bag, sealing the evidence.

'No, he's a cat but he looks more like an alien,' Clementine said, 'and he never goes to the toilet anywhere except his litter box. That's the truth.'

Mr Doncaster shook his head gravely. 'It's a very serious offence to find animal waste inside a public establishment. I need to know exactly where your pets are allowed to go.'

'Please, I can explain,' Lady Clarissa began. 'This has never happened before. I can assure you.' She opened one of the dining-room windows to air the room. 'Clementine, you and Aunt Violet run along and I'll see you both at dinner.'

'Mummy's telling the truth, Mr Doncaster,' Clementine said as she and her great-aunt exited the room. The pair of them almost barrelled over Ms Spencer.

'What were you doing?' Aunt Violet demanded. She could have sworn the woman had had her ear to the door.

Finley smiled sweetly. 'Hello there. I've just returned from the most glorious run – five miles around the entire village. It really is lovely out.'

'You must be a good runner,' Clementine said, impressed.

'Why, thank you,' Finley replied.

'Old people always get really sweaty and red in the face, but you look as if you've just had a shower and a stroll around the garden,' Clementine added.

Aunt Violet's lips contorted as she controlled a smile.

'You're a frank little thing, aren't you? I'll have you know I'm not *that* old,' Finley smirked. She gestured to the dining room. 'Is everything all right in there?'

'That's none of your business,' Aunt Violet snapped.

'There's no need for that sort of attitude.' Finley Spencer pursed her lips. 'I was just concerned. I thought someone sounded upset.'

Clementine tugged on her great-aunt's sleeve. The woman bent down and Clementine cupped her hand to Aunt Violet's ear. 'Please don't be mean to her, or she'll give Mummy a bad report too.'

Aunt Violet rolled her eyes and mumbled an apology, but there was something about the woman that didn't sit right with her. As Clementine pointed out, for someone who'd just been for a five-mile run, there wasn't a make-up streak or a hair out of place on their guest's perfectly coiffed head.

Finley Spencer strode away upstairs, muttering something about it being hard to get good service these days.

'Come along, Clementine, how about I go with you and the others for a walk?' Aunt Violet suggested. 'I don't think any of us want to be in the house for a while.'

Finley Spencer stopped on the landing as she listened to the old woman's plans. She'd be very pleased to have the house almost to herself.

SECRETS

Clementine panned the camera around the kitchen, where Basil, Ana, Aunt Violet and Drew were drinking coffee. Tilda, Teddy and Will were sitting at the breakfast bar enjoying mugs of hot chocolate.

'Please, Clementine, stop pointing that wretched thing at me,' Aunt Violet protested. 'I must look dreadful.'

'You look the same as always, Aunt Violet,' Clementine said.

'Well, excuse you,' the old woman huffed.

Clementine frowned. 'I meant you always look lovely.'

'Oh, that's all right then,' the old woman said.

Ana and Drew smiled at one another and Basil winked at them.

'Could we go into the garden and shoot some more scenes of Lavender playing soccer?' Clementine asked.

'That sounds like a marvellous idea,' Aunt Violet said. 'Off you go. Shoo!'

'I'll get the ball,' Tilda said, as she raced into the hallway to the stairs.

'Ask Mintie if she wants to play too,' Ana called after her. 'I think she's in her room reading.'

'Come on,' Teddy said to Will. 'We can take Flash, but I think he's going to have to be the cheer squad. He's too slow to be in the game.'

The boy picked up the tortoise from his little compound in the utility room, and Clementine beckoned Lavender to go with her. Pharaoh was sound asleep on the couch.

Within a couple of minutes the shouts of gleeful children could be heard in the garden and the adults were left to have a quieter conversation.

'Have you been through that box of photographs yet?' Basil asked Aunt Violet. 'I'd love to have a few of those pictures for the film.'

Aunt Violet shook her head. 'I'm afraid Clarissa has her hands full with Mr Doncaster's unexpected visit,' she replied. 'Leave it with me and I'll see if there are any you can use.'

'There is one thing I've been wondering,' Basil said tentatively.

Violet Appleby's face drained of all its colour. She hoped it wasn't the question she'd been dreading since Clarissa had agreed to him making the stupid film.

'Where is your daughter these days?'

'That's none of your concern,' Aunt Violet said sharply, 'and you're not to discuss it in the film, or I will make sure it *never* sees the light of day.'

Drew and Ana glanced at one another.

'I am sorry, Aunt Violet, I should have spoken to you privately,' Basil said.

'No, Basil, you shouldn't have spoken about it *at all*.' Aunt Violet took a large gulp of her coffee. 'I need to get going. Drew can bring Clementine.'

Violet Appleby walked to the sink and tipped the last of the coffee down the drain.

'Thank you, Ana,' she said quietly, and slipped through the door into the front hall, exiting the cottage as fast as she could.

Tears streamed down the old woman's face as she walked home. The last time she had seen Eliza was almost thirty years ago when, as an eight-year-old child, she had gone to live in Sweden with her father. Violet had tried to keep in touch but her daughter wouldn't reply to her letters or calls, and over time Violet had come to accept that the only person she had ever truly loved was gone from her life forever. She had no idea where Eliza was now, but that didn't mean she had disappeared from Violet's thoughts. On the contrary, there were days when it felt as if someone had torn her heart from her chest and replaced it with a frozen stone.

Clarissa had only ever mentioned her cousin once but Violet's explosive reaction had ensured that the woman would never do so again. Basil was bound to find the birth certificate – he was a documentary filmmaker after all. It was his job to do research and get the facts. This was just one fact Aunt Violet would have preferred he miss.

Clarissa looked up from where she was busy chopping vegetables for dinner. 'Hello Aunt Violet. Where's Clemmie?'

'She's still at Basil's,' Aunt Violet sniffed. 'Drew will bring her back later. I'm going to bed. My head is pounding.'

Clarissa wondered if something had happened. 'Mr Doncaster said that he's not going to record the earlier incident,' she reported.

'It took me quite a while to convince him that we've never had that problem before. Fortunately, the rest of the house was spotless apart from a pile of pencil shavings in the music room, which I'll speak to Clementine about when she gets back. And he would like Lavender and Pharaoh to come home so he can see how they behave in the house.'

'Good, good,' Aunt Violet said absently. 'Could you bring me some tea, Clarissa? I shan't be joining you for dinner, but I'll have googy-eggs and soldiers in my room at seven.'

Clarissa rolled her eyes. She'd telephone Basil to ask if Clementine and the others wouldn't mind bringing the pets home with them. She was also keen to find out if there had been anything odd happen while Aunt Violet was there.

The woman finished chopping the last carrot and wiped her hands on her apron. Uncle Digby was setting the dining table, having fumigated the room and scrubbed the patch of carpet where the offending item had been found.

Clarissa picked up the telephone and dialled Basil's number.

'Hello Basil, Clarissa here,' she said. 'Would you be able to send Lavender and Pharaoh home with Clementine? Our special visitor knows about them and he's asked to see them.'

There was a short pause as she listened to Basil. Clarissa then asked him if anything had happened with Aunt Violet.

'Oh dear, that explains a bit. There is one other thing,' she said. She had almost forgotten with everything else that had been going on. 'I had a look through those photographs and I think there are several you'll be able to use. But, even better, I found Granny's diary tucked in the bottom!'

There was a knock at the kitchen door.

'Sorry, Basil, I have to go. See you soon,' Lady Clarissa said before hanging up.

She walked over and opened the door.

'Hello, I was just wondering if I might get a cup of tea,' Finley Spencer asked.

Clarissa couldn't help thinking how attractive Ms Spencer was with her creamy skin and honey-coloured hair pulled back into a low ponytail. Dressed in dark jeans and a crisp white shirt, the woman looked as if she could have stepped straight from the pages of a magazine. Everything about her looked expensive – from the diamond-encrusted watch to the enormous emerald ring on her finger.

Clarissa wondered why Ms Spencer had chosen to have her holiday at Penberthy House. She looked like the sort of woman who'd have felt much more at home in a five-star establishment, not their funny old hotel. Clarissa pushed the thought away. It was none of her business, really, and who was she to complain about having house guests?

'Certainly, Ms Spencer. I'll bring it to you in the sitting room,' Lady Clarissa replied.

The woman was looking over Clarissa's shoulder as if searching for something.

'Can I help you with anything else?' Clarissa asked.

'Oh no,' Finley said, smiling sweetly, 'I'm just fascinated by big old piles like this one. I was keen to see what the kitchen looked like.'

'You're welcome to come in and have a look.' Lady Clarissa opened the door further, and in a blink, the woman had pushed her way inside.

'Ooh, may I have a peek in here?' Finley called, already helping herself to a tour of the pantry.

HOME

'**M**ummy, guess who we brought home?' Clementine rushed into the kitchen with Lavender skittering along the flagstones beside her.

'Hello darling,' Lady Clarissa replied. She walked towards the door to greet the rest of the entourage. 'Come in, everyone. I've just made a pot of tea.'

'I think Miss Appleby will be happy to have this one back,' Drew said, holding up Pharaoh's cat carrier.

The creature gave a yowl.

'Goodness, Pharaoh, what's that complaining about?' Clarissa smiled as Drew put the carrier down and unzipped the top. Pharaoh promptly jumped out and went straight to his food bowl.

Clementine turned around and saw Ms Spencer sitting at the kitchen table, a look of sheer terror on her face. 'It's all right,' the girl said. 'Pharaoh doesn't bite. He's just ugly.'

'I wasn't worried.' Finley smiled momentarily at the child, then turned to speak to Drew.

'I won't stay, Clarissa,' Basil said. 'I want to get back and start reading, if I may?'

Clarissa was glad to hear it. She really needed to get on with dinner, and she preferred to do so without an audience. 'I think you're going to enjoy it. Granny has some wonderful descriptions of parties and guests, and the most extraordinary thing is that the King once came for dinner.'

She handed Basil the diary and walked him to the back door, out of earshot of the others.

'I am sorry about upsetting Aunt Violet,' the man said after relaying what had happened that afternoon in more detail.

'She'll be fine,' Clarissa assured him. 'It's a touchy subject but we'll have to discuss it one day. I'll let her know you won't mention it in the documentary.'

'Absolutely,' Basil said before farewelling Clarissa and trotting off.

As Clarissa re-entered the kitchen, she was surprised to see Uncle Digby come through from the hallway with Mr Doncaster behind him. Uncle Digby was carrying a tray loaded with crystal glasses and champagne flutes, which he hurriedly placed on the bench near the sink.

'Oh, hello there,' Clarissa said, eyeing the tray. 'What can I do for you, Mr Doncaster?'

'Mr Pertwhistle said he saw Clementine returning with Lavender and Pharaoh. I'd like to meet them. I'm rather hoping to leave in the morning if I can finalise my report tonight.'

Finley Spencer's eyes widened.

Lady Clarissa's did too.

Uncle Digby spotted the look on their guest's face and wondered what that was about.

'This is Lavender,' Clementine said proudly, beckoning Mr Doncaster over to where the little pig was sitting in her basket by the range. 'And this is Pharaoh. They spend most of the time in this basket except when Lavender is outside playing soccer or going for walks to the village.'

Alfie Doncaster knelt down beside the pair. 'Well, Clementine, you were right about one thing. Pharaoh certainly is an unusual-looking creature.'

The cat sat up and arched his back, then began rubbing his head against Mr Doncaster's outstretched hand.

'But he's friendly enough.' The man picked up Pharaoh and began to sniff him all over. 'Mmm, he doesn't even smell like a cat.'

He put the creature down and turned his attention to Lavender, who began to playfully tickle his fingers with her tongue.

'Lavender loves having baths, doesn't she, Mummy?' Clementine said, eager to prove that there were no bad smells coming from her pet either.

Alfie leaned in and sniffed away. 'For goodness sake! You wouldn't credit it but I think she smells like her namesake.'

Clementine grinned. She wasn't about to tell him that Lavender had rolled around in Ana's lavender patch during their game of soccer.

'See, Mr Doncaster, I told you they were lovely,' the child said.

'I quite agree.' The man smiled at her. 'Well, I'm going to head up and start work on this report.'

'Yes, I think I'll have a shower before dinner,' Ms Spencer said. 'I must look a frightful mess.'

Lady Clarissa didn't think that at all. The woman was immaculate, but she was pleased to have the kitchen to herself.

'What are you and Will going to get up to, little girl?' Finley asked Clementine as she stood up from her chair.

The child was surprised that Ms Spencer was interested. 'We're making more of our movie,' she said, glancing at Will, who nodded.

'In the library?' the woman asked.

'No, in the kitchen,' the girl said. 'It's not Basil's movie. It's our one about –'

'How lovely,' the woman said with a patronising smile.

But before Clementine could finish, Finley Spencer was gone.

'Dinner's at half past seven,' Clarissa called after her.

'Come on,' Clementine said to Will. 'Let's get the camera.'

A HAIRY MESS

'Would you like a hand with anything?' Drew asked.

'Thank you for the offer but I should be back on track once I finish this pastry,' Clarissa said.

'I wish you'd have asked me a few minutes ago, then you could have been blubbering like a baby over here instead of me,' Uncle Digby sniffed, in the middle of chopping onions for the pasta sauce. He wiped his eyes with the back of his sleeve.

'I could wash those glasses,' Drew offered, spying the tray beside the sink.

Lady Clarissa laughed. 'Drew, you're a *guest*.'

'No, not at all. Think of Will and me as part of the family for the next week. We're happy to pull our weight around the house.'

The man donned a pair of pink rubber gloves and set to work. He turned on the tap and reached into the cupboard beneath for some washing-up liquid.

Clementine looked up from the kitchen table, where she and Will were reviewing their movie footage. 'You're dad's a good helper,' she said to Will.

'He must really like your mum because he usually hates washing up,' Will whispered.

Clementine giggled. 'I think my mum must like him too because she would never let guests help.'

Lady Clarissa looked over at the children. 'What are you two whispering about?'

'Nothing,' Clementine said, grinning at Will.

Lady Clarissa turned back to Uncle Digby. 'I was going to ask you about those glasses. Where did you find them?'

'It was the strangest thing,' the man replied. 'They were the glasses I put out for dinner this evening. I took them out of the cupboard and checked that they were clean, but when I went back to change the candlesticks I noticed that they all had lipstick marks on the rims.'

'Thank goodness you spotted it.' Lady Clarissa sighed. 'Mr Doncaster would have had a fit.'

Clementine nudged Will. 'What colour is the lipstick?' she said, climbing down from her chair and walking over to take a look.

Will held a glass in the air, examining it closely. 'It's a dark shade of pink,' he replied.

Clementine picked up another glass and narrowed her eyes at its stained rim. Will hurried over to join her. 'Aunt Violet wears lipstick that colour,' Clementine said quietly.

Will nodded. 'Maybe she's the one who's been doing all those strange things.'

Just as Clementine put the champagne flute back by the sink, a bloodcurdling scream rang out from upstairs.

Lady Clarissa dropped the rolling pin and Digby Pertwhistle sent a pile of onions flying off the bench.

'Heavens, I almost lost a finger!' the man exclaimed.

Drew whipped off his rubber gloves and raced upstairs with Lady Clarissa, Uncle Digby and the children right behind him. Just as they reached the top, there was another shriek.

'It's coming from the Blue Room,' Uncle Digby panted.

They ran along the hallway and found Mr Doncaster poking his head out of his bedroom door.

'What's going on?' the man demanded, scurrying out to join them.

Drew knocked on the door of Ms Spencer's room and turned the handle. 'Are you all right in there?' he called, tentatively poking his head inside.

The woman was standing in the middle of the bedroom dressed in a towel with another piled on her head. 'There's a monster in the drain!' she shrieked.

'What are you talking about?' Alfie Doncaster pushed his way past the others and headed straight into the ensuite. The rest of the group followed.

Lady Clarissa's heart thumped.

'The water wasn't draining properly, so I decided to have a look in the plughole. I'm quite handy, you know, and I didn't want to bother anyone,' Finley said between sobs. 'I started to pull and, oh, it was ghastly.' The woman shuddered dramatically.

Alfie and Drew peered into the shower. Within a flash Alfie produced a pair of latex gloves from his pocket and picked up the creature, placing it into the empty bathtub, where he could inspect it more closely.

'It's not a monster, Ms Spencer,' Alfie Doncaster concluded. 'It's a giant hair ball.'

'Oh, that's disgusting.' The woman touched her forehead with the back of her hand and looked as if she were about to faint.

Lady Clarissa's eyes widened at the sight of the matted mess. 'But I'm meticulous with my bathroom cleaning,' she said, dumbfounded.

Uncle Digby shook his head. 'I don't understand, either. I flush all the drains with Drain-O once a month.'

Clementine looked at the hair and then at Will. 'Someone cut off Nellie's hair,' she said.

'Who's Nellie?' Mr Doncaster asked. 'Don't tell me there's *another* pet.'

'My dolly,' Clementine said.

Lady Clarissa looked at her daughter. 'Clementine, did you do this?'

'No, Mummy. I promise I didn't,' Clementine said.

'That's not doll's hair,' Finley Spencer snapped. 'It's *human* hair, from all the guests that have ever had the misfortune to stay here. It's clear your mother is a terrible housekeeper.'

'No, she's not,' Clementine said crossly. 'And why did you take Uncle Digby's towel?' Clementine pointed at the monogrammed initials, DP, on the towel wrapped around Ms Spencer's head.

Finley Spencer's jaw dropped. 'Yuck! I thought this felt damp. What kind of dreadful place is this? Hair balls in the drains and staff towels given to guests – used ones at that.'

Uncle Digby gasped. 'Heavens, that *is* my towel.'

To ensure that the family's towels never got mixed up with those reserved for the guests, Lady Clarissa had had them all monogrammed with the owner's initials. For a second time that day, Uncle Digby wondered if he was losing his marbles. Surely he hadn't put his own towels into Ms Spencer's room.

'I suppose I won't be leaving in the morning after all.' Alfie Doncaster's brow furrowed. 'I'll need to do a full inspection of the drainage system and check on your laundry procedures tomorrow. Now, if you wouldn't mind handing over that towel, Ms Spencer, I'd like to run some tests on it.'

Finley Spencer's tear-stained face seemed to cheer up almost immediately as she whipped the towel from her head and handed it over.

'I'll get rid of that right away.' Uncle Digby was about to pick up the hair ball when Mr Doncaster blocked his way.

'No, you don't.' Mr Doncaster wagged a finger at the man. 'This is *evidence*.' He pulled a Ziploc bag from his pocket.

'Ms Spencer, you're welcome to use the bathroom in the hall,' Lady Clarissa offered. 'I'm –'

Finley Spencer shook her head. 'No, I'll wait for this one to be cleaned,' she insisted. 'Mr Pertwhistle won't be long, will he?'

'But you might catch a cold,' Clementine said to the woman.

'I'm fine,' she said sharply. 'Now, if you all wouldn't mind leaving . . .?'

SCARY SURPRISES

'That's so strange,' Clementine said as she and Will walked back into the hallway.

'Maybe your Aunt Violet did it,' Will suggested. 'She didn't come out to see what was going on, and Ms Spencer was *really* loud.'

Clementine frowned. 'Aunt Violet did say Mummy should sell the house . . .'

She hated to think that her great-aunt would do anything so horrible, but at the moment all the clues pointed right at her.

'Maybe we should see if her lipstick matches the glasses,' Clementine said.

Will nodded, and the two children dashed upstairs to the top floor. Clementine knocked gently on Aunt Violet's bedroom door but there was no reply.

'What if she's asleep?' Will whispered.

'We can just take a quick look,' Clementine said, determined to find out the truth. 'She always keeps her lipstick in the same place on her dressing table.'

Will gulped. His face was as pale as a snowflake.

'Don't be scared,' Clementine said. She turned the handle and poked her head inside.

Will followed her and, together, the pair tiptoed across the carpet to the dressing table, which sat under the window opposite the large bed. They could see the outline of Aunt Violet under the covers. She was fast asleep, her breaths punctuated by fluttery snores.

Clementine scanned the dressing table. 'It's not here,' she said. 'Someone must have taken it.'

The children turned to leave when, all of a sudden, Aunt Violet sat bolt upright in bed. Clementine and Will froze, then realised she was wearing an eye mask with two giant eyes painted on it.

'Eliza, darling, is that you?' Aunt Violet called out. 'Can you get Mummy a glass of water?'

Clementine wrinkled her nose.

'Who's Eliza?' Will mouthed.

Clementine shrugged and pointed towards the door. The two children scampered like mice on the balls of their feet. As Clementine turned to pull the door shut, Aunt Violet fell back onto the bed and began snoring like a train.

Most of the household was fast asleep when a loud ruckus shattered the evening peace.

'Good grief, get off me!' Alfie Doncaster shouted.

Clementine awoke to the man's cries. Digby Pertwhistle had just been having the most unsettling dream when he heard the commotion and sprang from his bed.

'I think it's Mr Doncaster,' Clementine said as she met Uncle Digby in the hallway.

They raced down to the Marigold Room. Alfie Doncaster burst into the hallway in his dressing-gown, his grey hair sticking up in tufts all over the place.

'I thought you said that the animals didn't go anywhere near the guestrooms,' Alfie barked at Clementine.

'They don't,' the child said.

'Then explain that there!' Alfie pointed to his room. Uncle Digby and Clementine hurried through the door, where they saw Pharaoh fast asleep on the man's pillow. 'You can imagine how I felt when I woke up to *that* curled around the top of my head! And I can't even wake the beast. Is he in a coma?'

'He's a heavy sleeper. I'll take him.' Uncle Digby walked towards the bed.

Alfie reached into his briefcase and pulled out a camera. 'Not until I have photographic

evidence to add to my report. Honestly, I have tried to overlook things I've seen here, and Lady Clarissa has done a wonderful job convincing me that they were all just anomalies, but I am beginning to think that the complainant was right. I am going to recommend that Penberthy House Hotel be shut down immediately, pending further investigations.'

'But we'll have to sell the house,' Clementine protested.

'If I were your mother I'd take the money and run.' Alfie Doncaster snapped away with the camera before giving Uncle Digby the nod to take Pharaoh.

'I don't want to sell the house,' Clementine said, her voice wavering. 'It's not fair. Pharaoh never comes up here, so someone must have put him in your room.'

'Show me the evidence and I'll reconsider,' Mr Doncaster huffed, and slammed the bedroom door.

Clementine and Uncle Digby took Pharaoh down to the kitchen.

'Do you think Mummy will really have to sell the house, Uncle Digby?' Clementine asked.

'I'm sure it won't come to that,' Uncle Digby reassured her, but truthfully things didn't look good at all. 'Now, come on, let's get back to bed.'

MOVIE AFTERNOON

The following day dawned grey and miserable, just like the members of the household.

'I'm so sorry you had to deal with all that last night,' Lady Clarissa said to Uncle Digby as the pair sat down to breakfast.

'Don't worry about me, Clarissa,' the man replied.

Clementine thumped downstairs, still half-asleep, in her dressing-gown and slippers. She yawned loudly, heralding her arrival.

'Hello sleepyhead.' Her mother stood up and greeted the child with a cuddle.

Clementine rubbed her eyes. 'What time is it?' She looked at the kitchen clock and realised that it was after nine. 'Oh no! I'm going to be late for filming.'

'No, darling. Basil telephoned and said that he's taking the day to go through Granny's diary,' Lady Clarissa said. 'You now have the day off.'

Clementine looked outside at the heavy sky. The rain didn't look as if it was going to let up anytime soon. 'Did Uncle Digby tell you about Mr Doncaster?' she asked.

'Yes, sweetheart.' Lady Clarissa pulled the girl onto her lap. 'Don't you worry about a thing.'

Clementine laid her head on her mother's shoulder. 'He said he was going to close our hotel.'

'That's for me to work out. Now, what can we do to cheer everyone up?' Clarissa said, tapping her chin.

'What about a movie afternoon?' Clementine suggested, perking up. 'Will can help me. Please, Mummy?'

Clarissa nodded. 'That is a great idea, as long as Drew doesn't have any other plans. He might like to take Will out on his day off.'

'Can you help me make popcorn, Uncle Digby?' Clementine asked. 'And can we invite Tilda and Teddy and Mintie?'

'I'm afraid that the children and Ana have gone to visit her mother today to give Basil some peace and quiet at home,' Clarissa said.

'Oh.' Clementine's face fell.

'But your mother and I will come along and watch, and I'm sure Aunt Violet would love to see your movie too.' Uncle Digby smiled at Clementine.

'If she ever wakes up,' Clementine said. She paused and then looked at her mother. 'Who's Eliza?'

Lady Clarissa flinched and Uncle Digby almost spat out his eggs. 'Where did you hear that name?'

'Will and I went to see Aunt Violet yesterday but she was asleep and I think she was having a dream and she called out for Eliza,' Clementine explained. 'Aunt Violet doesn't have any children, does she?'

'Oh, darling, please don't mention that to Aunt Violet. We'll talk about it another day.' Lady Clarissa glanced at Uncle Digby, whose face crumpled into a soft smile. 'You'd better hurry up and get dressed so you can organise your movie afternoon.'

'Did I hear someone mention a movie afternoon?' Drew asked as he and Will appeared on the back stairs.

Clementine turned around excitedly. 'Can you and Will help? Basil said we have the day off.'

'Yes, I just spoke to him. How about I finish editing your movie and we can watch that first?' Drew asked. 'Basil sent me the copy of your ballet concert last night too.'

Clementine grinned. She spotted the video camera perched on the edge of the dresser and raced to get it. She looked at the blinking red light, which indicated the battery was almost flat. 'Uh oh, I think we left this on last night.'

'Don't worry, Clementine,' Drew said. 'I can charge it.'

Clementine handed him the camera.

'We could make some posters, just like the ones for real movies,' Clementine said to Will.

The boy nodded eagerly. 'We could make tickets too and we could charge everyone a gold coin to watch.'

'And we could give the money to Queen Georgiana's Trust for the Protection of Animals,' Clementine suggested.

Lady Clarissa smiled at the children. 'Listen to you two. Filmmakers and philanthropists.'

'A philanthawhat, Mummy?' Clementine asked.

'It just means that you're generous, giving your money to others who need it more than you,' Lady Clarissa said.

'Oh, we could give the money to you, because you need it for the hotel,' Clementine suggested.

Lady Clarissa smiled at her daughter. 'That is very thoughtful of you, but I'd rather you give it to the animals.'

After lunch Clementine and Will finished setting up the library for the screening. 'Mummy, is Aunt Violet going to come down?' Clementine asked.

'I'm not sure, darling,' Lady Clarissa said. 'She hasn't been well.'

Clementine nodded.

The library looked just like a proper cinema with the chairs in neat rows. Uncle Digby had helped drag an old puppet theatre down from the attic, which Clementine and Will had transformed into a box office by the door. The retractable screen sat at the end of the room and the projector was positioned behind the seats. Several hand-drawn movie posters adorned the walls. The children had made tickets and positioned place cards on the seats too.

'Come on, everyone!' Clementine was doing her best to round up the members of the household, who kept on disappearing. 'Drew, you're sitting next to Mummy,' Clementine directed. She paused, looking around for her. 'Uncle Digby, where's Mummy gone now?'

'I saw her in the hallway with Ms Spencer,' the man replied as he poured fresh lemonade for everyone.

Clementine raced off to find her. 'Mummy, the movie's about to start,' she said, grabbing the woman's hand and dragging her down the hall.

'I'm coming, darling,' Lady Clarissa replied. 'What were you going to say, Ms Spencer?'

'I'm leaving this afternoon. Family emergency. I'll pack my things and be off in a little while,' the woman said breezily.

'Oh, I am sorry to hear that,' Lady Clarissa replied. 'I hope everything is all right.'

'Yes, better than all right,' the woman purred. 'I'm sure it will be fine.'

Ten minutes later Clementine and Will had sold six tickets in total – to Lady Clarissa, Uncle Digby, Drew, Lavender, Pharaoh and, most surprisingly, Mr Doncaster. Clementine eyed the man warily as he walked in and sat in the middle of the front row, where she had reserved a seat for Aunt Violet.

'This had better not be a trick,' Mr Doncaster complained.

'I can assure you, you'll love this,' Drew said.

Clementine handed each guest a bag of popcorn and a cup of fresh lemonade, although Lavender and Pharaoh would have to wait until they were back in the kitchen to have theirs. Then she stood in front of the screen with Will beside her.

'Ladies and gentlemen,' Clementine began, 'we are proud to present, for your viewing pleasure . . .' She looked over at Will and gave a nod.

'. . . *Beauty and the Beast*,' Will finished proudly.

Clementine giggled and nudged him. 'We're not calling it that, remember?' she whispered loudly. 'Aunt Violet will get mad.'

Will blushed as the audience tittered with laughter.

Clementine took a deep breath and started again. 'We are proud to present *Lavender and Pharaoh: An Unlikely Love Story*.'

The two pets had front-row seats, except they were sitting on the floor.

'Weren't you going to wait for me?' Aunt Violet sniffed as she strode through the door.

'Aunt Violet!' Clementine rushed to the old woman and hugged her around the middle. 'I'm so glad you're feeling better.'

'Settle down, Clementine. I just had a migraine. I wasn't about to die.' Aunt Violet made her way to a spare seat at the front, a smile at the corner of her lips. 'Besides, I was told I had to be here,' she said, glancing at Drew.

'Are you sure you're feeling okay? Clementine asked. 'You look different.'

The old woman frowned. 'Perhaps because I'm not wearing any lipstick. It seems to have gone missing.'

Clementine and Will shared a look before taking their seats.

With everyone finally settled, Drew pressed 'play' and the screen came to life. He hustled across the row of chairs to sit beside Clarissa. The movie started with a sweet scene where Lavender looked to be giving Pharaoh a kiss, followed by Lavender running about playing soccer and Pharaoh looking on lovingly through the Hobbses' window.

Clementine and Will took turns narrating the movie. Mr Doncaster chuckled at Lavender rolling about in Ana's lavender bush and there were some shots of the two creatures in the garden at Tilda and Teddy's house, which almost caused Aunt Violet to choke.

'What's my Pharaoh doing outside?' she demanded.

'It's fine, Aunt Violet. He was supervised,' Clementine said.

The movie continued with shots of the pair in the kitchen when all of a sudden the sound crackled and the screen went black.

'Is that all?' Aunt Violet said. 'What happens in the end?'

'Oh no, is this where I left the camera on in the kitchen last night?' Clementine said disappointedly.

'Trust me, Clementine, you'll be very glad you did.' Drew winked at her. 'I think you're all going to love what comes next.'

Clarissa and Uncle Digby looked at one another and shrugged.

'What's he talking about?' Uncle Digby asked.

The screen came back to life, this time showing a dim kitchen illuminated only by a couple of wall lamps. In the corner of the frame was an outline of a person – a woman. They all watched as the shadowy figure reached down into Pharaoh's basket and picked up the sleeping cat. Then she walked up the back stairs and vanished out of shot.

'Ms Spencer!' Clementine exclaimed. '*She* took Pharaoh upstairs.'

'Yes,' Drew said, 'and if you look at the time stamp on the video, it happened not long before Mr Doncaster discovered Pharaoh wrapped around his head.'

'Oh, dear me,' Mr Doncaster gasped. 'Drew, you were right. It seems we have a saboteur in our midst.'

Lady Clarissa looked at Drew. 'You knew about this?' she asked.

'I saw it when I was editing the footage this morning. I thought it best if Mr Doncaster found out with everyone else. I should have told you. I'm sorry,' he said sheepishly.

Clarissa shook her head and smiled. 'Don't be sorry. It's brilliant ... but Ms Spencer's leaving any minute now.'

'No, she's not,' the group chorused.

Drew jumped up and took off, with Lady Clarissa and the rest of the household hot on his heels.

GOTCHA!

They reached the entrance foyer just in time to see Finley Spencer bouncing down the staircase.

'Stop right there!' Drew yelled.

The woman paused and smiled like the cat with the cream. 'Hello Drew. Whatever's the matter?'

'I'll tell you what the matter is,' Lady Clarissa said, stepping forward. 'You've been caught on camera, red-handed.'

'What are you talking about?' Finley demanded.

'You put Pharaoh in Mr Doncaster's room,' Clementine blurted.

'I did no such thing.' The woman dropped her suitcase with a thud. At the same time a small gold cylinder fell out of her pocket. It clattered on the ground and rolled down the steps, stopping in front of Aunt Violet's foot.

'That's my lipstick!' Aunt Violet gasped, reaching down to pick it up. 'I've been looking for it everywhere.'

Finley Spencer gulped.

Clementine and Will looked at each other and then at the woman.

'You put the lipstick on the glasses,' Will said.

'And you cut Nellie's hair and dropped the cake!' Clemmie exclaimed.

'May I have my key back?' Uncle Digby held out his hand, glaring at the woman. Finley Spencer pulled it out of her pocket and threw it at him.

Mr Doncaster turned to Clarissa. 'It seems I owe you an apology. What I don't understand is why. What did you have to gain by doing this, Ms Spencer?'

Aunt Violet suddenly realised what it was that had been bothering her about the woman. 'It was you in the paper the other day. You're Finley Spencer from Spencer Industries, aren't you?' the old woman flapped.

'Oh my goodness,' Lady Clarissa sighed. 'You're the person who's been sending me all those letters asking to buy Penberthy House.'

'You made the anonymous complaint, didn't you?' Mr Doncaster added, his eyes narrowing. 'And I bet you found out when I was coming so you could be sure that I'd find all those dreadful things.'

Finley shrugged. 'Forcing the hotel to shut down would mean they'd have to sell the house.'

'Why do you want the house so badly?' Lady Clarissa asked, still puzzled. 'The house has hardly any land and it needs extensive renovation.'

Finley Spencer laughed. 'I wasn't planning to *renovate* it. I was going to put a bulldozer through it to make way for the road I need for the housing estate right behind you.'

'Over my dead body!' Aunt Violet snapped.

'Over mine too.' Clementine stamped her foot.

Lavender squealed and Pharaoh let out a mighty yowl.

'Right then, I suggest we call the police,' Mr Doncaster advised.

Lady Clarissa shook her head. 'I just want an assurance from Ms Spencer that all plans for your development will cease, or I *will* go to the police.'

'All right, all right,' Ms Spencer spat. 'Honestly, some people don't know a good deal when they see it. Can I get out of this dump now?'

Lady Clarissa pointed to the front door. 'Be my guest.'

Finley looked expectantly at Uncle Digby, then at her bags.

The man raised an eyebrow. 'You can carry them yourself, dear.'

The group watched as Finley Spencer stomped down the last few steps and out the front door.

'Thank heavens for the two of you and your movie-making,' Lady Clarissa exclaimed, hugging her daughter and Will.

Clementine smiled at Will and then at her mother. 'That wasn't movie-making, Mummy. That was movie magic.'

CAST OF CHARACTERS

The Appleby household

Clementine Rose Appleby	Five-year-old daughter of Lady Clarissa
Lavender	Clemmie's teacup pig
Lady Clarissa Appleby	Clementine's mother and owner of Penberthy House
Digby Pertwhistle	Butler at Penberthy House
Aunt Violet Appleby	Clementine's grandfather's sister
Pharaoh	Aunt Violet's beloved sphynx cat

Friends and village folk

Margaret Mogg	Owner of the Penberthy Floss village shop
Pierre Rousseau	Owner of Pierre's Patisserie in Highton Mill
Basil Hobbs	Documentary filmmaker and neighbour
Ana Hobbs (nee Barkov)	Former prima ballerina and neighbour
Araminta Hobbs	Ten-year-old daughter of Basil and Ana
Teddy Hobbs	Five-year-old twin son of Basil and Ana
Tilda Hobbs	Five-year-old twin daughter of Basil and Ana
Flash	Tilda and Teddy's pet tortoise

Others

Drew	Basil's sound engineer, hotel guest
Will	Drew's son, hotel guest
Alfie Doncaster	Health and Safety Inspector, hotel guest
Finley Spencer	Hotel guest

ABOUT
THE AUTHOR

Jacqueline Harvey taught for many years in girls' boarding schools. She is the author of the bestselling Alice-Miranda series and the Clementine Rose series, and was awarded Honour Book in the 2006 Australian CBC Awards for her picture book *The Sound of the Sea*. She now writes full-time and is working on more Alice-Miranda and Clementine Rose adventures.

www.jacquelineharvey.com.au

Look out for Clementine Rose's next adventure

CLEMENTINE ROSE

and the Birthday Emergency

1 July 2015

Puzzles, quizzes and yummy things to cook

THE CLEMENTINE ROSE

Busy Day Book

Out now